Dear Parent:

Your child's love of reading

Every child learns to read in a different way a
speed. Some go back and forth between reading levels and read
favorite books again and again. Others read through each level in
order. You can help your young reader improve and become more
confident by encouraging his or her own interests and abilities. From
books your child reads with you to the first books he or she reads
alone, there are I Can Read Books for every stage of reading:

SHARED READING
Basic language, word repetition, and whimsical illustrations,
ideal for sharing with your emergent reader

BEGINNING READING
Short sentences, familiar words, and simple concepts
for children eager to read on their own

READING WITH HELP
Engaging stories, longer sentences, and language play
for developing readers

READING ALONE
Complex plots, challenging vocabulary, and high-interest topics
for the independent reader

I Can Read Books have introduced children to the joy of reading
since 1957. Featuring award-winning authors and illustrators and a
fabulous cast of beloved characters, I Can Read Books set the
standard for beginning readers.

A lifetime of discovery begins with the magical words **"I Can Read!"**

Visit www.icanread.com for information
on enriching your child's reading experience.

ISBN 978-0-06-307798-0

Book design by Elaine Lopez-Levine

22 23 24 25 26   LSCC   10 9 8 7 6 5 4 3 2 1   ❖   First Edition

THE SMURFS™

Meet the Smurfs

HARPER

An Imprint of HarperCollinsPublishers

Meet the Smurfs!

They live together in Smurf Village.

They live in mushroom houses.

The Smurfs are small and blue.

They stand three apples high.

It may be hard to tell them apart,
but each Smurf is different!
They have different strengths.

Papa Smurf is the wisest Smurf.

He is the oldest and the smartest.

He solves big and small problems.

He always knows the answer.

All the Smurfs look up to him.

Smurfette is thoughtful.

She is also very curious.

She wishes the days had extra hours.

Then she could try more things!

When adventure calls,

she is always ready and brave!

Brainy is a know-it-all.

He thinks he's the smartest Smurf.

He reads a lot of books.

Brainy says he knows everything.

That's why he made himself

Papa Smurf's right-hand man.

Hefty is super strong.

He lifts weights every day.

He protects the Smurfs.

Sometimes Hefty can be a hothead.

He tries to use his brawn to help

his friends.

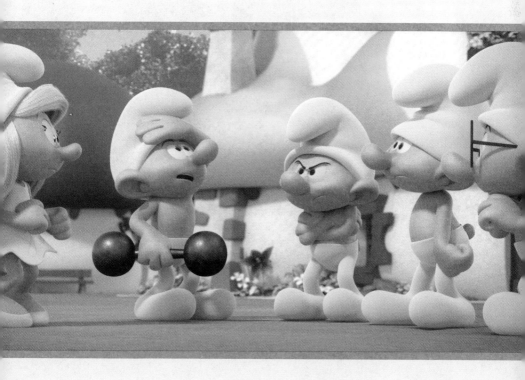

Clumsy is very clumsy.

He always drops things.

He trips over things.

Sometimes he even breaks things.

Clumsy is the kindest Smurf, though.

He is the best listener.

There's another Smurfs clan
called the Smurf Girls.
Their village is hidden
in the Forbidden Forest.

The Smurf Girls are independent.

They are strong and creative.

They love going on adventures too!

Smurfwillow is their wise leader.

She knows everything about plants.

She can even talk to them!

Smurfwillow is the Smurf

you turn to when you need help.

She sees the best in every Smurf.

Smurflily is super friendly.
She loves when the Smurfs
come together as a family.
She's there to lend a helping hand,
especially when there is trouble.

Smurfstorm is a fierce warrior.

She is an expert at archery.

The Smurfs are her family.

She is protective of them

and very loyal.

Smurfblossom is very enthusiastic.

She is friends with everyone.

She loves each and every Smurf.

Smurfblossom is full of happy energy.

She makes others smile

just by being around her.

Gargamel lives on the other side of the forest.

He is a crafty, evil wizard.

He wants to capture the Smurfs.

Gargamel sets traps for the Smurfs!

The Smurfs work together to escape.

Azrael is Gargamel's cat and sidekick.

When Gargamel's evil plans fail,

Azrael gets blamed.

Every day is different in Smurf Village.
No matter how big the problem is,
the Smurfs always stick together!

There are so many Smurfs to meet.

Some are jokey or grouchy.

Some are painters or chefs.

Each Smurf is smurftastic

in their own way.